Kimmy & Mike

To my wife Kim
Also to all the adventurous youngsters out there
Long may your big jib draw!
      ~ D.P.

To Adam and Eryn
      ~ L.S.-F.

KIMMY & MIKE

written by **Dave Paddon**
illustrated by **Lily Snowden-Fine**

It has often been said, and I can't disagree,

That there's no one as tough as our folk of the sea.

But two of the toughest, if the rights was known,

Were Kimmy and Mike, who lived in Belloram.

Now, one day late last fall, in a moderate gale,

In a 16-foot punt with a double-reefed sail,

They went to go fishing to their usual spot,

With orders from Mom: "Get something for the pot!"

Well, they caught a few sculpins and hauled up some kelp,

Tried a few different places, but nothing would help.

"Oh, my," said Mike, "looks like a dead loss."

"I know, now," said Kimmy. "Mother won't be some cross!"

"We'll try somewhere else," said Mike, with a sigh,

"Perhaps down around Nain or Ireland's Eye.

So, hoist up the sail so tight as a bar."

"Don't bother," said Kim. "I can scull 'er that far."

But the fish wouldn't bite and their luck surely stank

In the Gulf and the Straits and on Funk Island Bank.

"Let's try 'cross the pond," said Mike, with a smile.

"Alright, b'y," said Kim, "but you scull for a while."

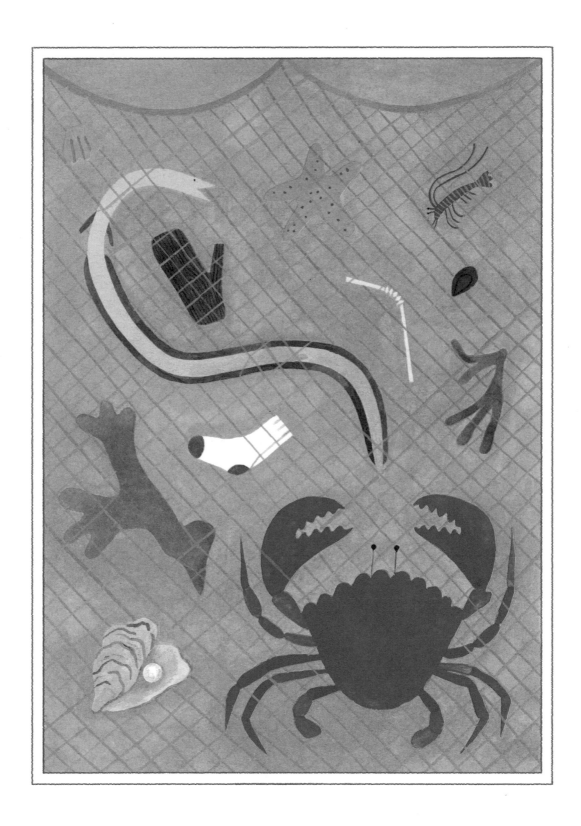

Well, two hours later they were anchored off France,

Having passed through two hurricanes, Alfie and Blanche,

With waves 60 feet and winds 90 knots—

Not too bad, thought Kim, a bit of a lop.

But there was nothing off France, and nothing off Spain,

'cept a small submarine that they threw back again.

While crossing the equator, they hauled up a squid

With 60-foot arms and a 30-foot head.

"Oh, my!" said Mike, "that's a giant one, I think!"

He had just gotten sloused with a puncheon of ink.

"Throw it back," Kimmy said. "Mother don't like them things."

But they cut off one arm for a meal of rings.

Off the Cape of Good Hope, they ran into a fog.

For two or three hours it was thick as a bog.

When it finally cleared up off some Antarctic bay,

A 100-mile iceberg was barring their way.

"Oh, my!" said Mike. "It's one thing, then another,

Trying to get supper for Father and Mother."

"Yes, b'y," said Kim. "I can't see a way through,

So pass up that axe 'til I cleaves 'en in two."

A short while later off the coast of Somalia,

They ran into some pirates who said, "We'll keel haul ya!"

Kim knocked out two dozen, one after another,

And said, "Go on home, b'ys, or I'll wake up me brother."

Next, they ran into a merman named Saul,

Who told them he wanted to visit Nepal.

"But they say you can't swim there," he said, with a sigh,

"So I guess I'll just sit here and blubber and cry."

"Don't be so sooky!" Mike said, on a rant,

"I'd like to visit the moon but I can't."

"I s'pose not," said Saul, and he cheered up a bit.

"I got a nice blowfish, if your mom would like it."

Politely declining the offer from Saul,

They rowed to Australia and set out a trawl.

Then they rowed 'round New Zealand and came back for a look,

But there was still nothing there that Mother would cook.

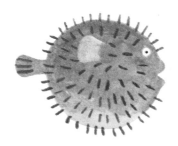

Off Hawaii they surfed on some 100-foot waves,

Won a prize, and got decorated with leis.

Eastbound once more, Kimmy said, "Look out front!

'Tis Mom! Coming out in Father's old punt."

"Now, where in the world have you young people been?

Your poor old father," she said, "what a sin!

He came all over sooky and started to sicken

When his supper was only a bucket of chicken."

"Sorry, Mom," said Mike. "There's not much on the go."

"Not much on the go?" she said. "No, I know!"

From the keel to the top of the thwart where she sot,

Her rodney was full of the fish she had caught.

She said, "Get on home out of it, through the Panama Canal,

And make your father his tea—you know he's not well.

I'm just going to dart 'round Cape Horn while it's light

And stop into Rio for bingo tonight."

Feeling slightly dejected, they both started rowing,

Not really watching out where they were going.

When all of a sudden, they ran hard ashore

On the Galapagos Island of San Salvadore.

"Oh, my," said Mike, "it's as hot as a sauna!"

"We don't call this hot," said a talking iguana.

"And don't get ideas 'cause I don't taste like chicken!"

Then, his speech got all slurred 'cause his forked tongue kept flicking.

So they shoved off again, and they headed northeast.

Mike said, "I hope we can get a few connors at least."

"We better get something," Kim said, starting to row,

"Or Mother won't give us some razzing, I know!"

A short while later, in the fading daylight,

The Panama Canal's western gate hove in sight.

"Not far now, bruddy," Kim said, with a grin.

But a sign said: "We're closed; please come back again."

"Oh, my," said Mike. "That's it!" thundered Kim.

See, they weren't supposed to be out after ten.

"Pass up that oar!" Kim said, with a roar,

"'Til I digs a way through to the Caribbean shore!"

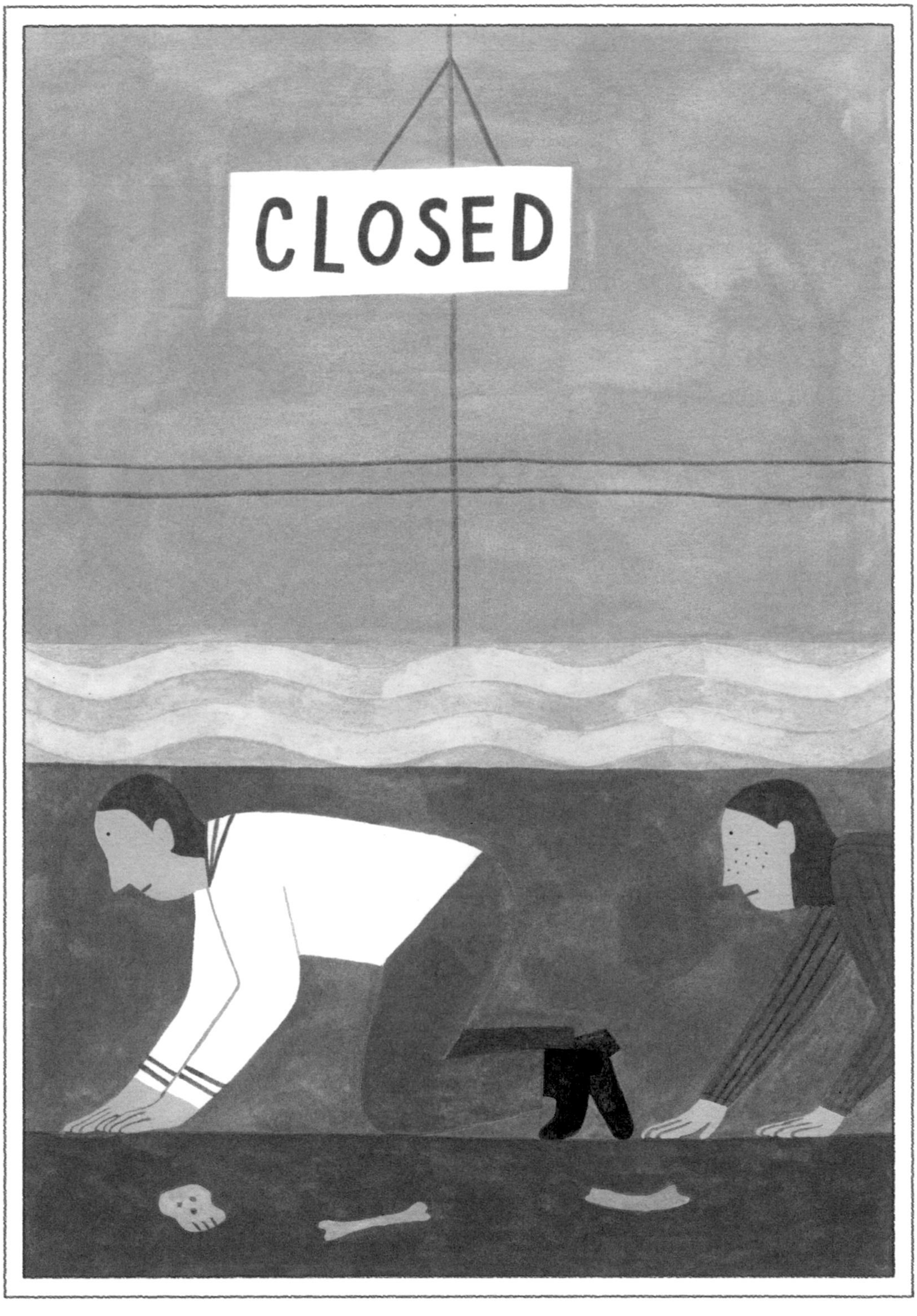
CLOSED

From that point on home the trip was routine,

And they were tied to the stage at about 9:15.

Father was crousty and wanting his tea,

And grumbling 'bout gas from that old KFC.

Next morning, their mother tied up to the wharf.

She'd won jackpot in Rio, then headed off north.

The fish she had caught was all salted and dried.

"Don't say you never got nothing!" she cried.

And so that's the story of Michael and Kim,

In Newfoundland and Labrador, they're average, but then

If it came to a racket I know that I'd druther

Tackle those two than tackle their mother!

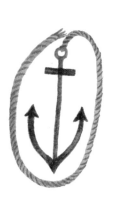

GLOSSARY

Bruddy: brother

Cleaves: splits

Connors: a small scavenger fish. (Slightly more desirable
　　than sculpins!)

Crousty: grumpy

Ireland's Eye: a re-settled fishing community in Trinity Bay.

Lop: a wave

Nain: an Inuit community in northern Labrador

Racket: a fight or argument

Razzing: teasing

Scull: to row with one large oar protruding from the stern
　　of a small boat

Sculpin: a bony fish covered in thorns. (Not what you want
　　to catch.)

Sloused: sprayed

Sooky: petulant

Stage: a wharf

Thwart: a seat in a boat. (Pronounced "taught".)

Tight as a bar: Taut, as in a sail filled with wind.

AFTERWORD

I don't know how far back the tradition of recitation stretches
in Newfoundland and Labrador history, but I'd guess four
or five hundred years. Our coastline was dotted with thousands
of isolated fishing communities—some of which might be home
to only one or two families, wresting a life from the sea. Music
featured prominently in the little bit of time available for rest and
recreation. But what if you had no instruments or no one could
play? Well, you always had your voice and your imagination,
and making up stories about your life, the supernatural, or your
neighbours was something available to all. Some of these stories
rhymed and were called recitations. Rivalries could be played out
this way, and it wasn't unusual to use a recitation to take a bit
of a dig at "buddy across the harbour". All in fun (maybe not
quite all…) and quite satisfying until a few days later, when buddy
had made up one about you! These duels could get lengthy
and personal, but were never the cause of open hostilities as far
as I know.

I'm happy to say that, after a few years of absence, the writing
of recitations is back with a vengeance here in Newfoundland
and Labrador, and new performers are emerging fairly frequently.
How good is THAT!!

~ D.P.

ACKNOWLEDGEMENTS

I would like to thank my wonderful publisher Marnie Parsons and Running the Goat Books & Broadsides. Marnie heard my first recitation and asked if she could put it in a book. "It can't be TOO bad," I reasoned. And now here we are, eight books later!

I would also like to thank Lily and Veselina for bringing the story to life.

~ D.P.

A retired airline pilot **Dave Paddon** is originally from Northwest River, Labrador. He grew up listening to the songs and stories of trappers, and attending late night "sessions" around many a kitchen table. He began writing his original recitations in 2007, and has now more than thirty to his credit, which he regularly preforms at festivals and fundraisers. Several have been published in print and audio format. Dave lives in St. John's, Newfoundland and Labrador.

Lily Snowden-Fine is an illustrator and multi-disciplinary artist living in Vancouver. Since studying at the Ontario College of Art and Design, she has illustrated three children's books for Thames and Hudson Publishing, as well as illustrated for such clients as the *New York Times*, the *Globe and Mail*, and Soho House London. She also has two upcoming children's books with Penguin Random House and Owl Kids.

This book was designed by Veselina Tomova of Vis-à-vis Graphics, St. John's, NL,
and printed in Canada.

978-1-927917398

Running the Goat, Books & Broadsides gratefully acknowledges support for its publishing
activities from Newfoundland and Labrador's Department of Tourism, Culture,
Arts and Recreation through its Publishers Assistance Program;
the Canadian Department of Heritage and Multiculturalism
through the Canada Book Fund; and the Canada Council for the Arts,
through its Literary Publishing Projects Fund.

Running the Goat
Books & Broadsides Inc.
General Delivery/54 Cove Road
Tors Cove, Newfoundland and Labrador A0A 4A0
www.runningthegoat.com